ORANGUTAN

by JON AGEE

Disney • HYPERION BOOKS

TONGS

Poems to Tangle Your Tongue

Cranky Oyster

What annoys an oyster?

What annoys an oyster?

You can find the easy answer in the *Post*.

A noise annoys an oyster,

A noise annoys an oyster,

And a noisy noise annoys an oyster most!

Wristwatches

I have a new Swiss wristwatch.

So does my old pal Mitch.

If you switched his wristwatch

With my new Swiss wristwatch,

Could you tell which wristwatch was which?

Felt Hat

I used to wear a felt hat, and I felt the hat felt right,

But I swapped it for a belt, although I felt the belt was tight.

Now, I've felt a lot of felt hats since I swapped it for the belt,

But I never felt a felt hat like the felt hat that I felt.

Purple-Paper People

There are people who use paper
That is colored only purple.
They are in the Purple-Paper People Club.
If you want to join these people,
First you buy a piece of paper.
Just be sure your piece of paper's purple, bub!

Rotten Writing

Reading writing

When it's written really rotten

Can cause your eyes and intellect to strain.

When it's written really rotten,

Writing's really rotten reading.

Yes, reading rotten written writing really is a pain.

Muesli

If you offer moose muesli,
They'll thank you profusely,
For muesli makes moose feel grand.
When feeding moose muesli,
Hold the muesli loosely,
To avoid getting nipped on the hand.

11

Walter and the Waiter

Walter Witter called a waiter: "Waiter, over here!

I want some water, waiter. *Water*, waiter! Is that clear?"

The waiter brought some water. Walter Witter shouted: "WRONG!

This water's really watered-down! I like my water strong!"

The waiter brought more water. Walter Witter was upset.

"This water's dry!" said Walter. "I like my water wet!

Bring me wetter water, waiter!" Walter Witter said.

The waiter brought a pitcherful and poured it on his head.

The Campbells

Eve and Ivan Campbell, over embers ably amble.

Over amber embers ably, they amble quite a lot.

If you were to stumble on the embers, you would mumble:

"Even Eve and Ivan's oven never gets this hot!"

The Surly Soldier

Should you shove a surly soldier
In the surly soldier's shoulder,
The surly soldier surely will turn red.
No, you shouldn't shove a soldier,
In the surly soldier's shoulder,
Or the soldier's sure
To hit you in the head!

Pink Kangaroo

"Grab a ball!" said the man. "Hit the pink kangaroo!"
Ann threw one. Wynn threw one. Juan threw one too.
"The prizes are all custom-made in Peru!"
Ann won one. Wynn won one. Juan won one too.

The Bubble

The world's biggest bubble-gum bubble
Was blown in the town of O'Toole
By a kid named Mark Anthony Hubble,
The bubble-gum champ of his school.
His teacher, Ms. Treacher, was speechless.
The class, it could barely sit tight.
For Hubble's improbable bubble-gum bubble
Was quite a remarkable sight.

Drawings

Drew and Lou drew drawings.

They both drew nicely . . . but!

Drew drew what Lou drew

And Lou drew what Drew drew,

So nobody knew who drew what!

Two Tree Toads

A three-toed tree toad tried to tie

A two-toed tree toad's shoe.

But tying two-toed shoes is hard

For three-toed toads to do,

Since three-toed shoes each have three toes,

And two-toed shoes have two.

"Please tie my two-toed tree toad shoe!"
The two-toed tree toad cried.
"I tried my best. Now I must go,"
The three-toed tree toad sighed.
The two-toed tree toad's two-toed shoe,
Alas, remained untied.

Peggy Babcock

Peggy Babcock at work. Peggy Babcock at play.

Peggy Babcock tomorrow. Peggy Babcock today.

Peggy Babcock, repeated, is tricky to say:

Peggy Babcock, Peggy Babcock, Peggy Babcock, olé!

Overeager Ogre

It isn't pleasant dining with an overeager ogre,

For overeager ogres often curse.

And it isn't wise to anger an overeager ogre,

For an *angry* overeager ogre's worse!

Camp

I dreamt I camped
In an unkempt camp,
Where the clothes were crumpled
And the tents were cramped.
It was so darn damp
That I felt contempt
For the unkempt camp
In the dream I dreamt.

This Zither

This is a zither, it has many strings.

Whenever I play it, a hummingbird sings.

Yes, I love this zither, this zither is fine.

This zither, this zither, this zither of mine!

Gus's Gas

Why does
everybody race
to buy their gas
at Gus's place,
especially when
the hill's so steep?
My guess is
Gus's
gas is
cheap.

Knapsack Straps

Nat bought a knapsack.
The knapsack looked right.
But the knapsack strap snapped
When Nat tied it too tight.
Nat bought a new knapsack strap
From the same store,
But the knapsack strap snapped
Like the strap snapped before.
Nat called the manager:
"This isn't right!
Your knapsack straps snap
When you tie them too tight!"
The manager nodded
And said with a wink:
"Our knapsacks are fine,
But our knapsack straps stink."

Mixed Biscuits

A box of mixed biscuits is always a treat.

Mixed biscuits are tasty! Mixed biscuits are sweet!

You offer mixed biscuits, and people will say:

"Mixed biscuits! Mixed biscuits! Mixed biscuits, hooray!"

Undies

There are lots of holes in Andy Bundy's undies.

His mom should get some thread and try to stitch 'em.

When Andy's at the beach, he's always cranky and upset,

'Cause Andy Bundy's sandy undies itch him.

The Dew Drop Inn

The Dew Drop Inn is a new Drop Inn.
The rooms are clean and cheap.
If *you* drop in at the Dew Drop Inn,
You'll have a restful sleep.
If *two* drop in at the Dew Drop Inn,
They'll get the discount rate.
So, *do* drop in at the Dew Drop Inn,
It's just off Highway Eight!

The Can't-Get-Inn

The Can't-Get-Inn
is
in
Berlin.
They built it
long
and
tall.
But it's so thin
you
can't
get
in
the Can't-Get-Inn
at
all.

Wacky Wheelies

Willy's really weary,
Willy's really weary.
He popped some wacky wheelies
With his friend Winona Stout.
Now Willie's on the sofa.
His wheelie days are over.
For Willie's wacky wheelies
Really wearied Willy out.

Les Moore

There is, more or less, more of Les Moore.

He looks bigger than he was before.

Though there're some who surmise

That he's still the same size,

There is, more or less, more of Les Moore.

Orangutan Tongs

An orangutan went into Wong's.

He ordered the pork and the prawns.

But he couldn't eat pork with a knife and a fork,

So they brought the orangutan tongs.

Orangutan tongs, orangutan tongs,

They brought the orangutan tongs.

The next day it happened at Kong's.

He ordered the *prunes* and the prawns.

But he couldn't eat prunes with a fork or a spoon,

So they brought the orangutan tongs.

Orangutan tongs, orangutan tongs,

They brought the orangutan tongs.

Dodos

There are very few things that a dodo'll do:

A dodo'll dawdle, a dodo'll diddle,

A dodo'll doodle a doodle or two.

A dodo'll yodel, a dodo'll coo.

But that's about all that a dodo'll do.

Notice

If you noticed this notice,
You'd notice this notice
Wasn't worth noticing,
so . . .
You needn't have noticed,
This notice you noticed.
It's time for this notice
to go!

ME

I Saw Esau

I saw Esau on a seesaw. Esau, he saw Lee.

Lee saw Esau's shiny tree saw; Lee saw Esau's tree.

Lisa, she saw Lee and Esau; she saw they were three.

I saw Lisa, Lee, and Esau, but none of them saw me!

ESAU'S TREE

ESAU

LEE
ESAU
LISA
3

LISA

LEE

ESAU'S TREE SAW

41

Hugh's Yo-yo

Hugh has a yo-yo,
A used yellow yo-yo,
He'll share his used yo-yo with you.
When Hugh isn't using
His used yellow yo-yo,
You can use Hugh's yo-yo too.

Thank You

I was thinking of thanking you,
as you can see,
I wanted to thank you
for thinking of me.
But now that I've thanked you,
I guess I am free
Of thinking of thanking you
thinking of me.

43

Unique New York

Unique New York, unique New York,
You know New York's unique.
You know you need unique New York,
You know New York is chic.

Unique New York, unique New York,
The crowded subways creak,
And people on the train are speaking
Spanish, Chinese, Greek.

Unique New York, unique New York,
You hardly need a week
To understand the reason why
New York is so unique.

45

Patty Petty

It's a pity pretty Patty Petty parted ways with Pete.

He was picky, partly portly, but particularly sweet.

They were such a pleasant couple as they pedaled down the street.

It's a pity pretty Patty Petty parted ways with Pete.

Fake Hiccups

When Herbert Hinkle hiccups,
His sister tries to too,
But mimicking him hiccupping
Is not easy to do.

Most of the poems in this book were inspired by classic English-language
tongue twisters, which I gathered from a variety of sources,
notably Alvin Schwartz's *A Twister of Twists, A Tangler of Tongues*,
(New York: J.B. Lippincott Company, 1972)